THE POPCORN MACHINE

by Hannah Grace

Once there were two brothers called Jack and Zach.

Their favorite thing to do was make popcorn to snack.

They made popcorn for dinner,
for breakfast
and even lunch.

Then in between meals,

they made popcorn to munch.

They brought popcorn to school to share with their friends.

They made popcorn bracelets to keep up with the trends.

Jack and Zach loved their popcorn and no other food.

Not even candy!

When they ate other food, they were in a bad mood.

One day Jack and Zach went with their mother to the store.

They could smell only popcorn when they walked through the door.

They followed the smell down an aisle of chips.

It was also packed with candy and crackers and dips.

They didn't care about all of the food on the shelves.

They never bought any food like that for themselves.

But at the end of the aisle was a new...

POPCORN
MACHINE!

They passed every gumball, every chip and Jellybean.

And stopped in front of the shiny, new machine.

Jack and Zach ran so quickly to see the price tag.

Then they ran back to their mom and they started to beg.

After begging and pleading,

She bought the machine that was shiny with chrome...

...And they started popping corn as soon as they got home!

Jack and Zach just kept popping until they ran out.

There were no more kernels, so they started to pout.

Jack and Zach were so hungry!

No other food would suffice.

Then Zach had an idea that just might turn out nice.

Zach ran to the fridge and grabbed handfuls of food
Then said, "Excuse me Jack, I don't mean to be rude."
"But if we can pop corn, then why can't we pop this?"
And he held up high a box of cheese that was Swiss.

Jack was shocked at Zach's suggestion to try something new.
But would it turn out yummy?
He really had no clue!

So they plugged in the machine and flicked the switch to "on"
Before their curiosity and faith was all gone.
Zach placed the cheese inside of the very top compartment.
And hoped that the result wouldn't ruin the whole apartment.

A FEW MINUTES LATER...
THE EXPLOSION WAS LOUD
and scared them to their knees!
But they found that it worked:
they had really popped cheese!

The pop-cheese was so good,
that they just had to try,
Something else from the fridge,
like brown bread or rye.

Jack popped carrots and yogurt
and oatmeal and juice.
Zach popped chicken and pizza
and even a goose.

The next day, they called all their friends to come taste
Their new pop-food, so none of it would go to waste.

Their friends gave suggestions of other foods they could pop.

Sally asked for pop-cake with a cherry on top.

Lily wanted pop-pie, pop-noodles and pop-rice.

Ted tried popping squash and it even turned out quite nice.

They ate all the pop-apples, pop-eggs and pop-gummies.

But alas,

All of this pop-food was upsetting their tummies!

Lily asked for pop-french fries, pop-limes and pop-yams.

Ted tried to pop cereal and even pop Jams!

They made pop-grapes and pop-peppers and even pop-fish!

If you asked, they would make you "pop-anything-you-wish!"

Jack and Zach and their friends had
eaten so much pop-food.
Their grumbling tummies put
them all in a bad mood.

Their friends knew it was time to stop all of this popping.

But the brothers did not listen;

They just were not stopping!

Jack and Zach got carried away. They went crazy!

At one time they even tried popping a daisy!

After popping a pear, the
machine started to smoke.

But they just kept on popping...

UNTIL IT
WAS BROKE!

Jack and Zach were so sad. that they started to cry.

Their friends wanted to help...

And they knew Just how to try!

Their friends unplugged the popper so nothing would burn

Then told Jack and Zach to wait for their return.

So they went to the store to look for a new popper.

Any popper would do, even one made from copper.

They had found a machine meant for food they could chop.

But Jack and Zach only ever ate food they could pop.

They looked high, they looked low,

But what could not be seen,

Was anything compared to a popping machine!

They were about to give up when they spotted a poster
With a picture of a bright and shiny new toaster.

They knew Jack and Zach liked eating
popped food the most.
But a food they must try
Was a nice piece of toast!

When the friends got back, the brothers were still crying.
So Sally said,

"CHEER UP!
WE HAVE SOMETHING
WORTH TRYING!"

She plugged in the toaster and threw in some bread.
And when it was all toasted she passed it to Ted.

So he spread on some butter and with that it was done.
Then he said, "See Jack and Zach, making toast can be fun."

The brothers each took a bite as all their friends stared.
To find out their reaction, they were all rather scared.

But the boys seemed to like it; Zach asked for some more.
And before too long, Jack ate more than four!

This became their new favorite and they even would boast.

And after that day,

They ate nothing but toast!

They made toast for dinner, for breakfast and lunch.

And in between meals they made toast just to munch.

Jack and Zach loved their toast, but no other kind of food.

When they ate other food they were in a bad mood.

They toasted bread all day. They toasted bread all night.

The thought of any other food just gave them a fright.

Until one day when Zach grabbed handfuls of food.
He said, "Excuse me Jack, I don't mean to be rude,"

"BUT IF WE
CAN TOAST BREAD,
THEN WHY CAN'T
WE TOAST THIS?"

And he held up high a box of cheese that was Swiss.

Jack was shocked at Zach's suggestion to try something new.
But would it turn out yummy?

He really had no clue!

ISBN

978-1-4602-3282-8 (Hardcover)

978-1-4602-3283-5 (Paperback)

978-1-4602-3284-2 (eBook)

Edited by:

Thelma Barer-Stein, Ph.D

Produced by:

FriesenPress

Suite 300 – 852 Fort Street

Victoria, BC, Canada V8W 1H8

www.friesenpress.com

Distributed to the trade by The Ingram Book Company

CPSIA information can be obtained
at www.ICGtesting.com
Printed in the USA
LVIC05n1629280414
383559LV00002B/24